CONTENTS

PROLOGUE

The sun was shining brightly on the shimmering lake next to the Summer Palace, but the tall woman had no shadow. She pulled her white fur coat around her as she glared across the water. Silently, a fox with three tails crept up to her side, its head bowed. She stroked it with her slender fingers, the nails long and

pointed, scratching the creature's back. "Soon, this will all belong to us," she said. The fox looked up at the Summer Palace, with its curved golden roof and whitewashed walls. All around, people were working and the small dock was busy with fishing boats.

The fox shook its head. "It doesn't look that great," he barked.

"Ah, but the Summer Palace isn't just a building," the woman explained. "It is the beating heart of all summer in the Jade Kingdom. When we conquer it I will have the power to bring an everlasting winter. The Dragon King will return, and revenge shall be mine!" The woman lifted her hands to the sky and let out a barking laugh. In the distance, more barking could be heard, echoing her laughter.

The woman in white fur, and her fiendish fox commander, began to walk towards the palace. As she passed the lake her true appearance glinted on the surface of the water – a white fox with burning yellow eyes, hungry for revenge.

CHAPTER ONE

Jack's hand twitched by his side like a cowboy in a gunfight as he stared at his opponent, whose glistening amber eyes glared back at him. Jack felt his heart thumping. The wrong move now could lose him the battle. Who was going to win? Him … or the massive tiger in front of him?

"I can do this, I can do this," he muttered to himself. He began to hop from one foot to another to psych himself up, jabbing the air in front of him with his fists like a boxer. He looked around at the hopeful eyes on the sidelines as the others all watched, holding their breath.

Can I do this? he thought – but before he had time to work out his next move the ferocious tiger leapt at him. Its jaws opened as it let out a mighty roar, revealing its sharp, glistening teeth. In that instant, Jack knew what he had to do!

He reached into his pocket for the coin he carried everywhere and flipped it high into the air. "ROOSTER!" he called, and a chicken suddenly appeared on his shoulder. Just as the tiger was about to

flatten him, Jack raised his arms and soared up into the air, using Rooster's magic power to fly!

They swooped above the garden and landed on a thick knobbly branch of a nearby tree. Jack's legs wobbled slightly as his trainers balanced on the branch, which was only as wide as his arm. He grabbed another branch to steady himself.

"Can't get me now, can you, Tiger?" he crowed as Tiger crashed into a flowerbed full of thorny roses. Jack looked down and grinned at the others.

Watching on the sidelines was an old man and a row of magical animals. There was Dog, Goat, Dragon, Ox – and all the other animals of the zodiac. And they all had a special skill, like Rooster's flying power. Jack waved down at them happily. Dog was laughing, Rat was whooping and cheering and nervous Rabbit was hiding his eyes under his paws.

"Next time you won't be so lucky!" growled Tiger, shaking dirt from his face.

Jack grinned. Tiger could be moody sometimes, but he was still the animal he had the closest connection to. After all, Jack was the Tiger Warrior, even if he still found it hard to believe.

No one would guess that he was the guardian of a magical world called the Jade Kingdom. His grandad, Yeye, had passed him down the magic coin that let him control the zodiac animals' powers – but Jack still had a lot to learn. He was getting better, though, and at least this time he'd got feather-brained Rooster to do what he wanted!

"Good work, Rooster!" Jack turned, looking to his shoulder where the bird had been just a second before. "Rooster?" Jack turned to see his feathered friend flapping frantically as he landed back on the lawn. Rooster clucked his way over to a yellow broken bucket in the corner and began pecking it.

And with him gone, Jack's ability to fly had gone too!

"Hey! Rooster, don't leave me stuck up here! It's too high ... come back up and help me down," Jack demanded, putting both arms around the tree trunk. He suddenly felt very high up!

"What goes up, must come down," laughed his grandad, Yeye.

Tiger began to laugh too. Yeye patted

the now not-so-ferocious beast like
a kitten. "Practice will make perfect;
it's not a computer game, Jack. You
can't press buttons and hope for the
best. You have to use your head a little
better. Think a few moves ahead of your
opponent," said Yeye.

Rooster had moved on to pecking
the door of the shed. Jack sighed. He
should have known better than to rely on
Rooster!

"Not bad, Jack," Dog shouted up at
him. "But you do know that running
away up a tree isn't going to help you
beat Tiger. Trees are only good for one
thing in my opinion." Dog lifted his leg.

"Dog! That is not well-mannered!" Goat scolded. All of the animals hollered with glee. Monkey did a backflip in delight.

"Dragon, can you fly up here and get me down?" begged Jack.

Dragon nodded her great head. She soared up and was by Jack's side in an instant. She picked him up gently and carefully glided back down, placing him on the ground next to Yeye and Dog.

"Thanks," Jack said, patting her scaly neck and feeling bad. He was training as hard as he could but he still wasn't anywhere near as good a Tiger Warrior as Yeye had been.

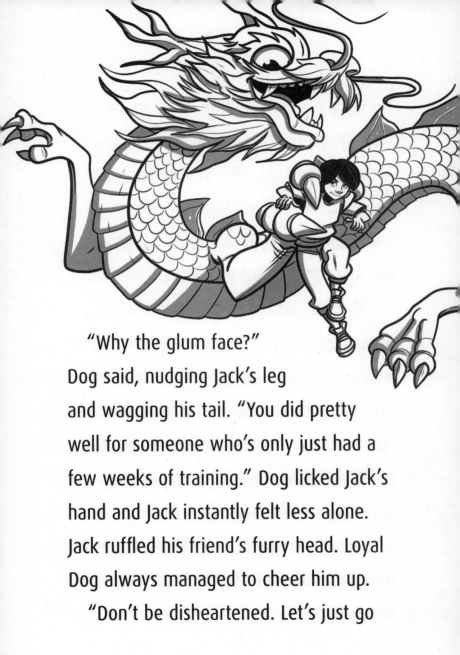

"Why the glum face?"
Dog said, nudging Jack's leg
and wagging his tail. "You did pretty
well for someone who's only just had a
few weeks of training." Dog licked Jack's
hand and Jack instantly felt less alone.
Jack ruffled his friend's furry head. Loyal
Dog always managed to cheer him up.

"Don't be disheartened. Let's just go

through it again. You'll get it, I know you will," Yeye said.

Jack sighed. Another training session on top of this one? "Argh! All we do is train. Can't I just go and visit the Jade Kingdom and hang out with Li? Please?"

"Not yet, Jack. Remember what happened last time – you need to be prepared," Yeye said, a serious look on his face. Jack had seen that look only a few times: when Yeye talked about Jack's father, who was no longer alive, and when Jack came back from his first visit to the Jade Kingdom and told him about his epic battle with the Dragon King. Yeye was worried.

Jack sighed again. "It's been so long since my adventure there! If I didn't have these guys" – he looked at the zodiac animals – "I'd think I dreamed it all!" *Did I really battle dragons and fight the Dragon King?*

"Adventure? You make it sound like one of your computer games. It's serious, Jack. You are the protector of the realm." Yeye began coughing, and stopped for a second to catch his breath. "The Dragon King has been waging war on the Jade Emperor and his kingdom for centuries, and his training and experience far outweighs yours. Come, another sparring session. Tiger, get ready for one more round."

Jack took out the Jade Coin. But as he brought it out of his pocket, he almost dropped it in surprise. The coin was glowing green, the engraved zodiac symbols on it all lighting up in his palm.

"Um, Yeye, something's happening!" Jack said. "Did you know it could do that?"

Yeye frowned. "Of course I did. The emperor is summoning you."

"He wants me to go to the Jade Kingdom?" Jack asked excitedly, butterflies bubbling around his belly. Dog barked happily and his tail began to wag.

Yeye sighed, putting his hands on his hips. "I'm afraid so. I was hoping you would be more ready."

The zodiac animals gathered round Jack. "We're ready when you are," Dog said.

Yeye gave Jack's back a pat and then stepped back, still looking worried.

"Don't worry, I'll be fine," Jack said.

"We'll look after him," said Dragon. The other animals nodded.

"OK," Yeye said, with a half-smile. "But you'll still have to do your training session when you get back. After all, time stands still while you are in the Jade Kingdom, so there's no getting out of it!"

Jack grinned back at him, then he flipped the Jade Coin into the air and yelled: "JADE KINGDOM!"

The Jade Kingdom needed him – he had to go!

CHAPTER TWO

As the magical coin spun in the air, a circle of light spiralled round and round. Through it, Jack could see forests of trees, with tall trunks and green sprawling branches. In the forest was a magnificent palace and next to it a calm lake with boats bobbing on the blue water.

Jack took a deep breath and then stepped through the circle, leaving his garden and grandad behind. The zodiac animals sprang though the portal behind him. Rat was first as always, scurrying forward excitedly. She ran up Jack's arm and peered over his shoulder, her nose scrunched up.

"Right, where can I get some fighting action?" she asked, eagerly.

Dog appeared next, shaking his head. "How can you think of fighting when there's so much to play with here? We could swim in the lake or find good sticks to chew in the forest ..."

"Speaking of chewing ... Pig, can you make sure this time you don't chew Princess Li's slippers!" Dragon said.

"They had cherries on top, how was I supposed to know they were made of fabric?" Pig snorted as he trotted out last, the portal closing behind him.

"It's so hot, I know you're all thinking it," Goat said, trotting up to the water's edge and placing her hooves in the lake.

"I'll cool you down!" Dog yelled, dive-bombing into the water and sending water splashing over Goat.

"Hey!" shouted Goat.

Jack would have loved to go for a swim, but he had to find out why the emperor had called him here. He scanned the horizon towards the huge palace. Nothing seemed wrong – it wasn't like last time, when he'd arrived to see a huge dragon blasting a village with ice. People had been running and screaming, trying to get away from the terrible beast; their homes had been destroyed. And that was before Jack had learnt the horrible truth – that the Dragon King had killed his father. His hands turned to fists as he thought about it. Jack had sworn to get his revenge.

"Are you OK?" Dog asked, looking up at Jack in concern.

Jack shook his head. "I don't know. Something isn't right. We need to find the emperor and Princess Li."

As if she had known he was thinking

about her, a colourful creature flew overhead, her black, green, red, white and yellow feathers floating behind like ribbons on a kite. It was Princess Li, flying in her magical form as the Fenghuang, the phoenix! Jack was so happy to see her. Not many people had a friend their age who could transform into a mythical bird and kick butt!

The animals saw her too as she flew overhead, and called out excitedly. Monkey jumped up and down, clapping his hands. Rooster flapped up into the air to see her.

The rest of the animals called out to the Fenghuang, and she turned rapidly

towards them. As she did, Rooster
bumped into her. The Fenghuang swerved
out of the silly bird's way, but as she
did her right wing bashed a tree branch,
causing her to lose control. She began
falling down, down, down and then crash-
landed at the side of the lake.

"Li!" Jack called,
racing towards her,
the animals running
behind him.

"Arghhh!" Li sat up
in her human form,
holding her arm.

"Li! Li! Are you
all right?" Jack

asked, worriedly. The animals gathered around. Dog nudged his way forward to the front of the rabble. Rooster clucked appologetcially next to Li and she stroked his feathers.

"Jack, it's you! Good to see you ... OWWWWW! I've missed you!" Li said. "Ouch!" She grabbed her arm and winced in pain. There was a large cut on her wrist.

"Use my power, use my power!" Dog barked excitedly.

Jack had never used Dog's healing power before. He put one hand on Dog's back and hovered the other over the cut.

"I hope this works," he said. Suddenly,

the blood began to stop dripping and the wound started to close up. Jack watched in amazement as Li relaxed and the pain left her face. The wound was now totally healed, just a line of new pink skin showing where it had been. "Sick!" Jack grinned.

Li grabbed Jack and gave him a big hug. "Thanks!" she said. "And thank you, Dog!" She ruffled his fur and his tail wagged happily.

"If my fur wasn't black as night, I'd be as red as a tomato!" grinned Dog.

"Even if your Rooster did cause me to fly off course in the first place!" Li joked.

"It's good to be back," Jack said,

looking up at the palace towering over the lake. "Where are we?"

"That's the Summer Palace! I was meant to find you and give you an official tour, not crash into the ground!" Li laughed.

"Is the Dragon King back? Is that why I've been asked to come here?" Jack asked as he felt his body tense. The Dragon King had escaped into another realm, but the emperor had warned that he would return. And when he did, Jack would have to face him.

"No, thank goodness. Nothing like that. You are here as the very special guests of my father. He's told me to invite you to his ..." Li looked unhappy.

"To his wedding ..." chimed in Goat.

"Goat!" Li yelled.

"Sorry about that," Jack said. "Goat, stop reading people's minds, it's rude!"

"I'm so sorry," Goat said anxiously.

"It's, OK, Goat, I know you can't help it," said Li.

"So, your dad is getting married again?" Jack asked. Li nodded. She didn't look that happy about it. "I'd feel weird if my mum got remarried too," he said sympathetically.

"Yinmei seems nice enough," Li said. "It's just something feels ... off. I can't explain it. But I'm glad you're here."

Suddenly, a gong rang out from the Summer Palace and Rabbit hid behind Li's leg. He pulled his ears down in case there was another loud noise.

"Come on, we need to join the pre-wedding celebrations," said Li, speeding up to the palace.

Jack and the animals followed. As they got closer to the palace there were more and more people, and by the time they got to the main gate there was hardly any room to move. Jack turned to the animals. "You'd better go back in the coin," he said.

"No fun!" complained Monkey.

"I want to see what's going on," said

Rat. "It's not fair."

"I could climb on top of everyone's heads and get to the front in no time," Monkey added, jumping up and down.

"Not now everyone, you can come out later, I promise," said Jack. "Now everyone back into the coin!" he said. The animals disappeared into the coin. Li grabbed his arm and they moved through the crowd.

"Oops, sorry," Jack said as he almost stepped on the trotters of a Dangkang, a green boar-like creature with big tusks. Its beady eyes blinked, then it made a loud snorting sound which seemed to alert everyone around. The crowd turned and saw Jack and Li. People moved back and whispers began spreading. Jack felt himself blush as he heard them mutter "Tiger Warrior". Instantly a clear path formed for him and Princess Li.

Jack was being patted on the back by smiling well-wishers, and many were bowing to Li as she passed beside him. Jack felt like a pop star. Back home he was invisible, but here he was a hero. It was a lot to take in.

They reached the front of the crowd just as the Jade Emperor stepped on to a tall green platform surrounded by local citizens and magical creatures. There were some that Jack recognised from

the myths Yeye had told him – like the
lion type creature stretched out by the
emperor's feet: that was a Pixiu – but
lots of others he didn't, like the group of
strange ducks that kept flapping at each

other. He made a mental note to ask Yeye about them when he got home.

Li joined her father up on the platform, while Jack stood to the side.

"Thank you all for coming; it is a very special day," the Jade Emperor declared. Li looked down at her feet. "I have gathered you all here to make an announcement. One that I hope will fill your hearts with joy as it has filled mine." The people looked on excitedly.

The Jade Emperor held out his hand. A very tall and elegant woman in a white fur coat took his hand and walked onto the platform. Her long, silvery-white hair reached all the way down her back.

"This is Yinmei, my bride-to-be! She will be the new Empress of the Jade Kingdom." The Jade Emperor grinned broadly. Li, on the other hand, was kicking the toes of her shoe into the floor. Jack felt sorry for her. It must feel strange to have new a step-mum around.

As the audience applauded, Jack felt the coin in his pocket grow hot, and Dog appeared next to him.

"What are you doing—" Jack stopped abruptly when he saw the look on Dog's usually friendly face. He sniffed the air, and his tail shot up. The hairs on Dog's back bristled as his hackles rose and he bared his teeth.

"Grrrrrrrr!" growled Dog, his body tensed as if ready for a fight. "What's going on?" Jack felt his face going hot with embarrassment. "Dog! Stop being so sensitive! If this is a joke, it's not very funny!"

But Dog wouldn't stop growling. "HOME!" Jack commanded. *Dog has never acted like that before*, Jack thought. Something was terribly wrong!

CHAPTER THREE

The Jade Emperor waved regally as he led
a colourful procession inside the Summer
Palace. Jack had sent Dog back into the
coin and no one had noticed his strange
behaviour except Yinmei, who had fixed
Jack with an amused smile. Now she
lingered behind to talk to Jack and Li.

"You must be the famous Tiger
Warrior?" she said, her voice light and

playful. Jack didn't know whether to bow or not. He still had a lot to learn about the Jade Kingdom.

"Hello, er ... yes, I'm Jack. Thanks for inviting me to your wedding," Jack said. The woman towered over him as she held out her hand.

"I am Yinmei. I'm very pleased to meet you, Jack. Li has told me all about you being the sacred guardian of the kingdom." Jack shook her hand and noticed her silver, talon-like nails. Her grip was strangely strong as well. "That is such a responsibility for someone so very young," she added.

Jack wondered how much she knew

about the Jade Coin and the zodiac animals. "I've got lots of friends to help me," he said, his fingers touching the coin in his pocket.

Yinmei smiled. "Yes, I know what you mean. It's good to have friends. I am especially happy that many of my own friends are coming to the wedding. I'm sure you'll

meet them all later," she said, putting her bony fingers on Jack's shoulder and giving it a squeeze.

"I just don't like her!" Li muttered as Yinmei walked away.

"Neither does Dog." Jack told her about his reaction. But before they could talk any more, they were swept into a huge banqueting hall, which was covered in ribbons of red and gold for the wedding the next day. Signs of 'Double Happiness' were placed all around to wish double the amount of joy to the newlyweds, and the tables were piled high with all kinds of food that made Jack drool just to look at it. There was

lobster and chicken, roast duck and even
something that looked like shark's fin
soup. At the end of the table there was a
huge pile of steaming sweet buns.

The emperor opened his arms wide
and silver fireworks shot up into the
air. "My friends!" he bellowed. "Let us
feast!"

Jack lay on top of the huge four-poster
bed. It was bigger than his whole
bedroom at home! Heavy blue fabric
hung from the ceiling around the bed.
Outside, the moon glittered on the lake.
"I'm so full!" Jack moaned as Tiger

climbed on the bed next to him. He'd never eaten so many courses in his life. "I ate more buns than Pig!" It was a good thing the bed was so big, since it looked like all the zodiac animals were going to be sleeping in it with him. He and Li hadn't had chance to talk at all, so Li had told him to stay at the palace – and Jack, not keen to go back to another training session with Yeye, had agreed.

The zodiac animals were mostly sleeping. Pig was snoring with his face in a bowl of oranges; Horse stood by the window with her eyes closed but her tail swishing. Dog was lying at the bottom of the bed. Jack could tell Dog was dreaming because he kept making a whimpering sound. Jack had tried to talk to him at the party, but all Dog would do was snap and growl.

Despite feeling tired, Jack kept replaying the things he had seen at the party. The circus performers twirling overhead, flying through the air holding long silks; a parade of great creatures – his favourite being a dragon whose movements left a neon glow in the dark. After that there had been fireworks over the lake that lit up the sky with explosions of colour – pinks, purples, whizzing sparkles of golden fire that flew through the air and reflected in the water.

It was all too exciting; he couldn't sleep. He lay looking up at the ceiling. There was something about Yinmei that got under his skin. She reminded him of one of the stories Yeye used to tell him, but he couldn't remember what it was.

As he lay in the dark, he heard a strange sound outside his room, like the pattering of paws. Jack fumbled in the dark for the Jade Coin, which was on his bedside table. He held it in his hand and used the glow to look around. Snake unwound herself from her spot by his feet and slithered up to him.

"Can't sssssleeep?" she asked.

"I heard a funny noise," Jack said.

"There are many people in the palace," Snake told him.

"I know. I think I'll just have a look around," said Jack, putting the Jade Coin into his trouser pocket.

"Do you want Dragon to come? She has been here many times and knows this place well," Snake said, looking over to where Dragon was asleep, lying on the floor like an enormous dragon-skin rug.

"No, don't disturb her. I just want to have a look around. But since you're awake, let's use your invisibility in case the guards don't want visitors walking about this late." Jack held out his wrist for Snake to coil around. As she did, Jack

felt her power surge through him and he began to disappear.

Unseen, Jack strolled through the halls of the palace. There was no one around and no sign of the animal he'd heard. He came across a huge door that was ajar, and he pushed it open. The moon streamed in through the windows, making it almost as light as day. Jack looked around excitedly. He was in a huge library with wooden shelves filled with books from floor to ceiling. Jack brushed his fingers against the spines of the books. Perhaps reading would help him feel tired and he could get some sleep? Snake unfurled from his wrist, making him visible again.

Jack picked up a large red book with gold binding and went to sit at a wooden table, well-lit by the moon. He looked at the Chinese characters on the cover and tried to remember the Mandarin Yeye had taught him. It was called MYTHS AND LEGENDS OF THE JADE KINGDOM. Jack began to flick through. The book mentioned many of the creatures and stories that Yeye had told him about. *Maybe I could find those strange duck-like creatures from earlier?* Snake slithered along the table to take a look at the book too. Then suddenly Jack saw something that made his heart beat fast.

On the page was a picture of white fox

with a crafty face – and next to it was a
picture of a beautiful woman.

"Snake, look at this creature. The Jiu
Weihu – a fox demon!" His heart pounding
in his chest, Jack read aloud:

*The nine-tailed fox can shapeshift into human
form, transforming into a man or a woman
using enchanting magic.*

They can bewitch those they wish to conquer.

*Their goal is to steal qi energy, the life force,
from their victims and make them weak.*

Jack shivered. "You don't think—" His
voice trailed away. "Yinmei had a big
white fur coat ..."

"It wasssss hot to be wearing fur," said
Snake, getting a close look at the picture.

"But Yinmei couldn't be a fox demon, could she?" Jack asked. Snake looked at him, and Jack jumped to his feet. "I have to tell Li!"

All of a sudden the window shutters slammed, and the doors to the library shut with a bang. The library was plunged into darkness. At the same time, a movement caught Jack's eye. He turned as something stirred in the shadows. Two yellow eyes gleamed in the pitch black.

CHAPTER FOUR

Jack sprang up and pulled out the coin. "ZODIAC!" he yelled. The other animals appeared by his side, rubbing sleep from their eyes.

"What's going on?" Goat asked. "I was dreaming about a meadow full of grass."

"Ssshhhh!" said Snake. "Jack needs our help."

"Someone or some*thing* is in the room

with us," Jack whispered. The zodiac animals were suddenly wide awake. They lined up, hoping to be called upon. Jack didn't know who his enemy was yet, so choosing which zodiac animal to help him was going to be tricky. He would have to wait for whoever it was to make the first move.

Jack held on tightly to the Jade Coin. Then suddenly more and more pairs of eyes appeared in the darkness like shining stars. Then the creatures began to wail, a noise unlike anything Jack had ever heard before.

"WAKKKKKKUUUUUOOOOOO!"

"Foxes!" screamed Dog. His fur bristled

and he bared his teeth. This time Jack
understood why he was so upset. Jack
wondered if he should use Dog's power.
He knew Dog hated the foxes, but his
power was healing. What good would
that be?

Jack could feel Tiger nudging his hand
and suddenly he knew what he needed
to do.

"TIGER TRANSFORM!" he yelled. He felt
the spirit of the Tiger meld into his body –
and his body stretched and twisted as he
turned into a tiger!

Jack stood in the middle of the room.
His tiger eyes were much better in the
dim light than his human ones, and

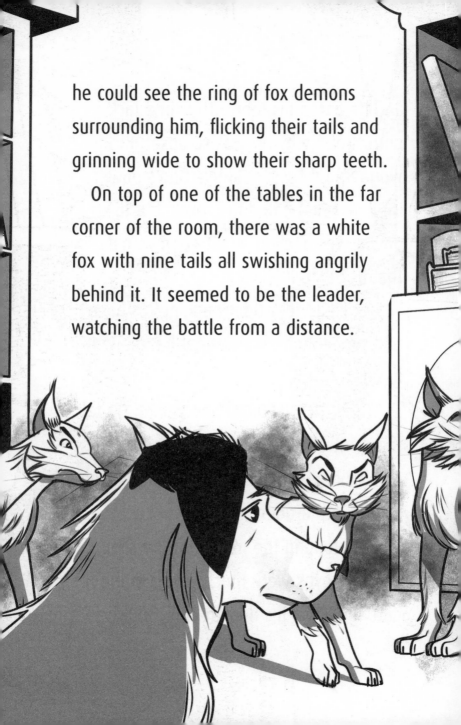

he could see the ring of fox demons surrounding him, flicking their tails and grinning wide to show their sharp teeth.

On top of one of the tables in the far corner of the room, there was a white fox with nine tails all swishing angrily behind it. It seemed to be the leader, watching the battle from a distance.

Suddenly it gave a bark, and as one all the foxes attacked, springing through the air towards Jack.

With a flick of his tail Jack blasted fire at the foxes in front of him. One leapt through the flames and landed on Jack's back, sharp claws tearing at his tiger fur. Jack roared in pain as he flung it off and quickly sent a sphere of fire after it. But the fox was quick and ducked out of the way, and the fireball smashed into a window, burning a hole though the shutters and melting the glass like butter. Moonlight poured into the room, making it easier for Jack to see the foxes all around him.

"Jack, look out!" Dog yelled as a fox pounced from behind. This time Jack leapt out of the way and the fox's needle-like teeth snapped at thin air. More and more foxes were appearing out of the corners of the room.

The nine-tailed fox gave another barking command. Without missing a beat Jack twisted and blasted a fireball

at it. It leapt to the ground, but Jack's fireball hit its paw. The fox stamped out the flames, howling in pain.

"We have to keep them away from the princess and the emperor," Dragon said.

Jack nodded his tiger head. He leapt through the broken window out into the courtyard. Looking back, he could see the foxes were following, just as he had wanted. Jack turned and headed for the forest as fast as his tiger paws would take him.

He heard the cries of the foxes behind him, the shrill barking piercing the night. Then he saw them all – a horde of red and white foxes, hundreds of them, and they were all chasing after him, their teeth glinting in the moonlight.

CHAPTER FIVE

Jack stopped running as he reached the lake. He'd led the foxes away from the Summer Palace, but now there were so many of them and only one of him. Even with Tiger's fire power, he didn't think he could take them all out, there were just too many. He raised his tiger paw and sent fireball after fireball into the pack, but however many of the foxes he fought off there were always more.

Just then a three-tailed fox broke free of the others and charged at Jack. Its sharp fangs snapped at his stripy side, drawing blood. Another fox sprang and bit his front leg. Jack tried to pull his attacker off, but the fox's yellow eyes

were fierce and determined as it tore at Jack's flesh. Jack roared and stamped his paw, shaking the fox off. But as soon as he got rid of one fox, another three were ready to attack. Jack had to think.

"HORSE!" he shouted, and a second later he was back in his human form and Horse was standing next to him. "Let's get out of here." Jack struggled up on to Horse's back as the foxes lunged and snapped at his ankles. He held on for dear life as she galloped through the woods, her lightning speed soon leaving the army of foxes behind, baying and barking.

Finally, they were safe, in a clearing

high on a hill overlooking the Summer
Palace. Still clutching his injured arm,
Jack slid off Horse's back and patted her
side. He and Horse stared down at the
Summer Palace, which was now shrouded
in darkness – apart from hundreds
of glowing yellow eyes circling the
courtyard.

As Jack looked at the menacing lights
he suddenly felt woozy and dropped to
the ground. His arm was sore from the
bite and blood was dripping from a deep
gash.

"We need healing power," neighed
Horse gently, and disappeared back into
the jade coin.

Jack groaned as he clutched his bleeding arm.

Seconds later Dog bounded forward. "I'm here, Jack, but you'll have to help!" he barked.

Jack laid one hand on Dog and put the other over the injured part of his arm. Dog closed his eyes and in an instant Jack felt a wave of warmth flow over his body. The skin around his cuts tightened and then began to tingle. It felt like being tickled.

Jack laughed as the warm heat from Dog's power spread into every cell of his body. It was like pure light was coursing through him, from the top of this head to the tips of this toes.

One wound after another healed in quick time. "Healing complete!" Dog barked, his tail wagging happily.

"Thank you, Dog," Jack said in relief. "I'm sorry I didn't listen to you earlier."

Dog leaned in as if he was going to say something, then licked Jack's face from chin to forehead.

"Bleurgh, Dog!" Jack laughed. He was glad he and Dog were friends again. He stood up and gazed down the hill towards the Summer Palace.

"Foxes, hundreds of foxes ... so Yinmei isn't alone – she has a whole fox army," Jack realised. "We have to tell Li and the emperor. But how?"

"You should rest," Dog said. "You still need to recover your strength. They aren't going anywhere." Jack looked down at the yellow eyes. It was true, they weren't moving – they were waiting.

"If Yinmei wanted to kill Li she'd have done it by now. She wants to be empress and steal the whole kingdom. We won't let that happen," he said. But Dog was right, for now there was absolutely nothing he could do.

Dog curled into Jack's lap as the Tiger Warrior leant against Ox and began to close his eyes. It wasn't the grand bed from the Summer Palace, but it was actually really comfy. Jack fell asleep listening to Dog's soft snores.

Cock-a-doodle-doo! Jack woke up to see Rooster standing on Ox's back, crowing at the sunrise.

"We can't stay out here," said Jack, looking down at the palace. "We need to stop the wedding." The animals nodded. Jack climbed on to Horse's back and the rest of the animals returned to the coin.

Jack rode like the wind back to find Li.

As Jack and Horse clip-clopped into the courtyard a tall figure was waiting there, a horrible smile on her beautiful face. She was wearing a red wedding dress with a white fur collar, the same as the fur of the nine-tailed white fox from the night before. Jack had a sudden thought, and looked at her hands. Sure enough, Yinmei's left hand was bandaged with white gauze. Jack's eyes widened. Yinmei was the nine-tailed fox he'd wounded last night in the battle!

"Ah, Tiger Warrior," she said. "The library has been destroyed in the night, a pesky problem with an intruder, but it won't affect today's Wedding Tea Ceremony, after which I shall become empress." She glared at him, and for a second he saw a flash of her fox eyes.

"Jack, there you are!" Li shouted as she appeared in the courtyard. Jack felt a surge of relief that she was OK.

"I'll see to you later— I mean, I'll see you later," Yinmei said, smiling. Then she swept away towards the palace.

Li rushed over, wearing a beautiful purple tunic embroidered with phoenix feathers. "I was looking all over for you. Where have you been?" she said breathlessly.

Jack pointed after Yinmei. "You were

right.
Yinmei
is here
to cause
trouble.
She's a fox
demon; she
and her army
attacked me
in the night."

"A fox
demon?" Li gasped. "Of course! She's
going to drain my father's life force so
he's too weak to fight!

"We have to tell him," Jack said. But Li
shook her head.

"He won't believe us. He'll think
I'm just jealous that she's not my real
mother."

"We'll have to make him believe us!"
said Jack. "We'll get her to turn into a fox
in front of him."

"But how?" Li asked.

"I've no idea!" said Jack. "But we have
to stop her!"

CHAPTER SIX

As Jack and Li raced into the palace
looking for the Jade Emperor, more and
more people arrived for the wedding,
wearing fine clothes and chattering
happily as they went to the throne room.
Among the guests were people who
looked like Yinmei, tall and regal with
high cheekbones and red or white hair.
Jack stared at two tall men as they swept

past, and one glanced at him, his eyes glinting with flecks of yellow when they caught the light of the sun.

"Are they … ?" Li murmured.

"Fox demons." Jack nodded. "They must be." Even in their human form you could tell once you knew what to look for.

As Jack and Li brushed past the newly arrived guests and headed to the Jade Emperor's throne room, Rooster suddenly appeared from the coin. Yinmei's guests all stopped and turned at the same time. It was eerie. They looked like they wanted a tasty chicken dinner. Jack quickly bundled Rooster into his arms and whispered, "HOME!" Rooster disappeared back to the safety of the coin, and the odd guests turned and carried on with their business.

The throne room felt colder than usual. Jack shivered. The ceilings were draped in golden ribbons, and huge statues lined the walls. Yinmei and the Jade Emperor were on the raised stage, which had been decorated in reds and golds, and a table was laid for the tea ceremony. Yinmei's guests had taken their seats and the Jade Emperor was already pouring the tea. Li ran up to the front of the stage.

"You've started the Wedding Tea Ceremony without me?" she said angrily.

Yinmei stood up, her face serene. "It is not your father's fault, Li. We knew you were with Jack ... and, well, I'm afraid I have to tell you that he is responsible for the destruction of our beautiful library. I have been advised that those born in the Year of the Tiger ..." Yinmei gazed at Jack, "are unlucky for our union. His presence here is a bad omen. He must leave."

Jack felt a flash of rage. Yinmei was trying to turn the emperor against him!

"Father, I need to talk—" Li started, but the emperor raised a hand.

"Tiger Warrior, if Yinmei says you should leave, then I respect her decision." The Jade Emperor looked different. His eyes were glazed over, his face thin. Yinmei had already been stealing his power! Yinmei poured tea too and as she did, Jack saw the bandage on her hand again. It gave him an idea. He walked over to Yinmei and bowed low. "Of course, I will leave if you want me to. But, Empress, I notice that you have injured your hand. As my parting gift on your wedding day, may I get my trusted friend Dog to heal it for you?" Jack bowed again.

The Emperor perked up. "Yes! That is a marvellous gesture. Thank you for understanding, Jack." He turned to Yinmei. "Come, my dear, let the Tiger Warrior heal you."

Before Yinmei could think of an excuse, Jack flipped the Jade Coin in the air and called out, "DOG!" Dog appeared at Jack's side.

Jack put a warning hand on his back. "Don't growl!" he whispered. Dog bristled, but he listened. "With Dog by my side, I can place my hand over your hand and heal it," Jack announced as he moved towards Yinmei.

"No! Get that creature away from me!" Yinmei flapped her unburnt hand at Dog.

"There's nothing to be afraid of," the emperor said. Jack and Dog took another step closer. Yinmei was climbing up the back of her chair, bristling with fury.

"Get this creature away from me!" she screeched again.

Dog leapt forwards, and as he did Yinmei stood up on the throne. "ENOUGH!" she bellowed. "I'm tired of playing this game. I wanted to be empress, but I will be content with taking this palace! If you want a battle, I will give you one!" She gestured with her arms and instantly all of her guests barked. The Jade Emperor, Li and Jack covered their ears to block out the terrible sound. Yinmei raised her arms again and suddenly she disappeared. Now, in her place, a large white fox with nine huge tails sat on the throne. Yinmei was in her true fox-demon form!

She swiped at Dog with one claw and he fell back, snarling. Yinmei grabbed the Jade Emperor and buried her claws deep into his chest. Jack watched in horror as the life force began to drain from the emperor's face. Then suddenly he turned

pale and fell to the floor.

"No!" shouted Li. She rushed over to her father. "Open your eyes, Dad!" The white fox pulled out her claws and leapt on to the stage, giving another harsh barking cry.

One by one the guests with the white streaks in their hair began to fall on all fours, their bodies shaking as they too transformed into foxes.

"Come, my army! Take over the palace!" Yinmei screeched. The room was full of foxes; they began attacking the other guests, who ran screaming, trying to escape.

The white fox laughed as she looked

down at the emperor. "Once you took
my land, the forests that I had grown up
in, and built this summer palace for your
own family. Now I shall claim it back and
turn this land into a forever winter, as
it used to be. And when I summon the
Dragon King, he will reward me mightily.
Finally, I shall have my revenge!"

At that, all the other foxes lifted their heads and filled the room with an eerie howl.

CHAPTER SEVEN

At Jack's feet the emperor moaned softly.
"The Dragon King!" he groaned. He was
far too weak to fight. If the Dragon King
came back now, he'd win for sure. Jack
glanced at Li and saw she was thinking
the same thing. They had to stop Yinmei
from bringing him back!

As Jack looked at the fox, wondering if
he could take her down, he noticed that

around her neck she wore a small purple jewel. Jack recognised it from his previous battle with the Electric Dragon. It was a summoning jewel – she could use it to call the Dragon King!

Before he could even move, the white fox lifted up the jewel and pressed its middle with her large white paw. Bright lights flashed and a diamond-shaped portal the size of a dinner plate opened on the other side of the room. Through it, Jack could see the face of his mortal enemy – the Dragon King. Anger rose inside his chest. He had never hated someone so much in his life.

"We can't let him attack while my

father has no power," Li gasped. Jack looked up and saw the portal beginning to widen. He had to do something to stop the Dragon King entering. They couldn't hold off all these foxes AND the Dragon King too.

Jack stood up tall and pulled the coin from his pocket. "OX!" he shouted, and the mighty Ox appeared next to him. Jack jumped on Ox's back and they charged towards the portal. Jack slid off Ox's back but leant his shoulder against Ox's side to make the connection – he'd need both his hands free for this. As Ox's strength filled his body, Jack put one hand on each side of the portal and held it tight, trying to shut out the evil figure peering in from the other side.

"Young Tiger Warrior!" laughed the Dragon King. "I wondered when I might see you again." He laughed as Jack strained, using all of Ox's strength to keep the magic portal from opening any more. "You weakling! You are nothing like the previous Tiger Warriors. You are a mere fly, a pest!"

Jack shouted over his shoulder to where Li was cradling her father's head. "I need your help! Smash the jewel!" he yelled, pointing at the white fox. Li nodded. She gently laid down her father's head and whirled into the air,

transforming into the Fenghuang, the mighty phoenix.

The Fenghuang dived down towards Yinmei, flapping her strong wings at the fox demon's face. The fox lost her balance and the Fenghuang snatched the purple jewel with her claws. She squawked with delight – but it wasn't over yet. Several foxes were chasing her, leaping up into the air and snapping at her colourful tail feathers.

"Jack!" she cried as one caught her by the tail. "Catch!" She lobbed the shining jewel into the air. Jack let go of the portal and caught the jewel. Then he channelled even more of Ox's power and, with a bellow, he crushed the jewel to powder in his hands.

"NO!" the Dragon King yelled as the portal began to shrink again.

"Who's a pest now?" Jack smirked, watching the portal disappear into thin air.

A terrible screech rang around the throne room as the white fox wailed.

"Dragon King! My master!" she shrieked, then turned to Jack in fury. "You might have stopped me from bringing back my master, but this palace is still MINE!" With that, the white fox leapt down from the stage and ran out the door. Her fox army followed her.

Jack and Li ran over to the Jade Emperor, who was lying on the floor with his eyes closed. His hair had turned grey and his skin was as dry and wrinkled as an old man's. His breath was faint.

"He's still alive, but barely. What can we do?" she asked. He no longer seemed like a demigod, but someone old like Yeye, someone whose years had caught up with him.

"Dog!" called Jack as he held out the coin. Dog appeared. Jack put one hand on Dog's back and held the other over the Jade Emperor, like he had before with Li. But even though the healing power poured into the emperor, he didn't get any better. Jack looked at Dog, who was shaking his head sadly. "He has lost a lot of life force. I don't think I can help."

"Can't you transform into Dog?" Li begged Jack. "Aren't you more powerful then? Maybe you could help him."

Jack felt awful. "I've only learnt how to transform into Tiger," he said. *If only Yeye were here. If only I were a real Tiger Warrior!*

"Try!" Li said, a tear falling down her cheek.

Jack held on to Dog and tried to clear his mind. How had he transformed into Tiger? He'd been calm and confident, like Tiger was. He tried to be as confident as possible. *I AM THE TIGER WARRIOR!* he thought, as hard as he could. But nothing happened.

Snake slithered in. "Foxesssss are attacking all of the wedding guests," she said.

"We need to get everyone to safety," said Jack.

Li pointed out the window to the boats at the dock of the lake. "We can go to the Jade Palace. The quickest way is across the lake."

Jack nodded.

Li turned to the nearest guard. "Get everyone to the lake!" she commanded, sounding powerful. "But I don't think my father can walk," she added to Jack in a quieter voice.

Jack summoned Horse. Together he and Li lifted the Jade Emperor up on to Horse's back.

They went out into the palace corridors, where all around foxes were snapping and chasing the wedding guests. A palace servant was climbing up a curtain as a fox snapped at his heels. Jack used Tiger's power to send a blast of fire at the fox, who ran away, snarling and spitting as he went.

"Thank you, Tiger Warrior," the servant said as he climbed down, looking wobbly.

"Follow us!" Li called to everyone they

passed. Jack shot fireball after fireball, clearing a path out to the lake, leading all the people with them.

As soon as they reached the lakeside, Li turned to the crowd, sounding every inch a leader. "EVERYONE! Listen to me. I urge you to flee in the boats out on to the water. We'll be safe there from the foxes. They have taken the Summer Palace. We must get to safety now!" Everyone began scrambling to find a spot in one of the wooden boats. Horse knelt so that Li and Jack could help the emperor into an imperial boat.

"Where am I?" the Jade Emperor asked as he opened his eyes, bewildered.

"Down at the lake, Father. But rest now – we're getting you back to the Jade Palace," Li reassured him.

The Jade Emperor turned and looked at the Summer Palace in horror. Jack followed his gaze.

All along the battlements, red foxes took up post. Yinmei stood victorious on the steps.

"No, I won't go! We have to go back to the palace," the emperor said, trying to get on his feet.

"Don't worry, we'll get the palace back – but not now, you need to rest," Li said.

"No, you don't understand." The Jade Emperor struggled to speak. "The

Summer Palace isn't just a building, it is the heart of all summer in the Jade Kingdom. If it comes under Yinmei's control then she will be able to destroy summer and usher in an everlasting winter! The whole realm will be frozen over – for ever." He sat up and grabbed Li and Jack with his bony hands. "You have to stop her!"

Just then snowflakes began to fall from the sky. Jack wrapped his arms tightly around his body as an icy cold wind blew through the entire land. The winter had already begun!

CHAPTER EIGHT

Jack and Li propped the emperor up under a tree as they watched the boats sailing across the lake. "At least the people are safe," said Li.

"I think you spoke too soon," said Jack. "Look!" The white fox and her army had arrived at the shoreline. In a whoosh, Yinmei transformed back into her human form. She spread her silver nails and Jack

noticed a thick white layer of ice starting to cover the lake. It spread faster and faster. The water on the lake was becoming solid white ice. The boats were going to be trapped! Then the fox demons stepped on to the frozen lake. Soon there was an army of foxes running over the ice towards the boats, their mouths open hungrily.

Jack looked at the people in the boats, rowing desperately as the ice spread towards them. "We need to help them!" he gasped.

"I can't leave my father!" Li said, holding the emperor's frail hand.

"Leave it to me and the animals," Jack said. "ZODIAC!" he shouted, holding out the coin. The twelve animals of the zodiac appeared one by one.

Rat was first on to the ice, but she slid and fell. "Come back here, you cowardly foxes!"

Jack looked at her and wondered if her weather power could help. Maybe some sun would melt the ice? But it would take too long! Then what about Dragon's water power? But Dragon was already shaking her head.

"I can't do much with the water already turned to ice," she said.

Tiger came forward and nudged Jack's hand.

"OK, Tiger, let's send them some firebolts," Jack said, his hand on Tiger's back. Tiger roared, and fire pelted into the air and down on to the ice. It made small holes, making some foxes fall on their faces, but many more still headed towards the boats full of people. Jack saw Yinmei laugh. It was up to him to stop her. But how?

"The Jade Emperor ... you must restore his power first," Dragon said. "Only then can the foxes be defeated."

"But I have to save the people on the boats!" Jack said, looking back at Li as she cradled her father's limp body. What should he do? Stop the fox attack, or try to save the Jade Emperor?

Dog rushed to his side, teeth bared. "Let me get those foxes, Jack," he growled.

Jack looked down at Dog. He just couldn't get used to seeing his fun and friendly Dog so angry. Dog snarled as a fox came close.

Wait! Jack thought suddenly. Maybe

Dragon is right. We need to focus on the Jade Emperor. We need a new strategy. Sometimes when I'm gaming I have to think outside of the box. If I want to defeat a Big Boss in a game, I have to gain more tools to help me. We need to heal the Jade Emperor, then he can defeat Yinmei!

"I hate those foxes so much!" Dog's ears were pulled back, his teeth bared as he growled.

"Oh Dog, I hate seeing you so upset," Jack said. Dog hadn't been himself ever since the foxes arrived.

"I know, it's not me. It's those foxes!" Dog growled.

Jack suddenly had an idea. He'd been able to transform into Tiger when he'd been calm and confident like him – when he'd understood Tiger's spirit. But Dog wasn't confident and calm – he was loyal and funny ... suddenly Jack had an idea. "Dog ... what do you call a fox with pears in his ears?"

"I don't know," said Dog.

"Anything you want – he can't hear you!" Jack laughed. It felt good to smile again.

Dog laughed too.

Jack started clowning around, trying everything he could think of to make Dog laugh. He pulled funny faces, told jokes and even did handstands.

Li turned to him from where she was cradling her father, her face streaked with tears. "What are you doing?" she said angrily. "The foxes are attacking my people, and my father is dying!"

Jack pretended not to hear her as he started to fall over, then did a forward roll. It might seem silly, but Jack knew his friendship with Dog was the thing he had to focus on, not the hundreds of foxes heading for the boats. He finally understood Dog's spirit. He just hoped it would work.

"Hey Dog, what type of markets do dogs avoid? Flea markets!"

"Good one, Jack!" said Dog, laughing so hard that tears fell down his face. Jack held tightly on to Dog's body and hugged his friend hard.

Dog relaxed. And in that moment it happened – a powerful light entered Jack's body. It surged through his hands, and the tingling sensation that he had

felt when he had healed his own arm was magnified a thousandfold. Healing power surged through his core. Jack felt his tongue hang out of his mouth happily and his tail wagged.

He had transformed into a dog!

CHAPTER NINE

Jack barked happily as he celebrated turning into dog form. But there was no time to play. He bounded over to the Jade Emperor.

"Jack? Jack, you did it! Can you heal him?" Li asked.

Jack put his paws against the Jade Emperor's chest, where the white fox had pierced his body. Bright yellow light flowed through Jack to the emperor. Closing his eyes, Jack felt healing energy surge through his paws.

At first nothing happened, then slowly the colour returned to the emperor's skin and he began to move. His hair turned from grey back to black and the wrinkles on his face smoothed out.

Li gasped as her father's life force flowed back into his body. "It's working!"

Jack took his paws away and waited, holding his breath.

The Jade Emperor gave a great gasp, and sat up, looking as strong as ever. "Thank you, Tiger Warrior," he said, bowing his head. It had worked!

As Li and her father hugged, Jack turned to look at the boats – and his heart sank. On the lake was a desperate scene. The foxes had made it across the ice and were snapping and snarling at the people in the boats, who were desperately fending them off with the oars. And standing on the lakeside, laughing with glee, was Yinmei.

"Emperor!" Jack barked. "We need your help!"

The Jade Emperor gave a great roar and thunder crashed in the sky above. Yinmei caught sight of him and started backing away, but there was nothing she could do. The Jade Emperor was back to his full power – and he was furiously angry.

"Come on, Jack, let's get those foxes,"
Li said, grinning in delight. As the Jade
Emperor walked towards Yinmei, lightning
crackling from his fingers, Li transformed
into the Fenghuang and soared into the
sky, ready to fight! She swooped down on
the foxes, taking them out one by

one in an aerial attack.

Jack wagged his tail as he bolted on to the ice. When the foxes saw the huge magical dog coming for them, they ran into the forest, yelping as they fled.

"You might have stopped me this time, but the Dragon King won't stop until he

rules this kingdom!" Yinmei screeched.

"And we'll be ready for him!" the Jade Emperor replied, sending a lightning bolt across the frozen lake into Yinmei's heart. The blast of light destroyed her instantly.

"The Summer Palace is safe once more," the emperor announced. The storm clouds lifted and the warmth of the sun blazed down, thawing the ice. The Fenghuang flapped her wings to make a wind that blew the boats back to the Summer Palace dock.

"Whoa!" Jack cried as the ice under his paws started to melt. Then he felt Dog's mischievous energy and belly-flopped straight into the water. "Well, I did want to have a swim!" he laughed.

The rest of the zodiac animals appeared on the shore, waiting for Jack to doggy-paddle back. When he came out of the water, he turned back into his human form. Dog stood next to him and shook his soaking-wet fur, drenching everyone!

"Dog!" Li shouted as she wiped water from her face.

"Thanks for making me laugh, Jack," said Dog, wagging his tail. "I didn't like feeling angry all the time."

Jack patted his fun four-legged friend on the head. "It's nice to have you back!"

One by one the boats returned and Jack and Li helped the people onto the dock.

Then they turned and looked up at the Summer Palace. All around it, icicles were melting off the trees as the leaves began to blossom once more.

The Jade Emperor smiled and turned to his people. "Thanks to the Tiger Warrior, the fox demons are defeated. Come, everyone. We may not have a wedding but there is still a banquet to eat! Let us celebrate."

Jack grinned at the thought of more sweet buns, but he shook his head. "I think I need to go home," he said. He had been away for days, but back at home it would only be a few minutes.

"Thank you for coming, Jack. You were

the only one who believed me and you helped save my father, again!" Li held out her palm and Jack high-fived it. "The Dragon King was wrong, you know, when he said the other Tiger Warriors were better than you. I'm sorry I doubted you." Li hung her head. "You transformed into Dog exactly when you needed to, and in time you'll master all the zodiac animals' powers. So don't worry."

Jack smiled back. It was just what he needed to hear. With that, he took the Jade Coin from his pocket, flipped it into the air and commanded, "HOME."

In a flash, Jack was back in his garden. Everything was exactly as he'd left it.

"Are you ready for your next training session?" asked Yeye, who was sitting in a deck chair.

"I've had enough real-life training to last me a lifetime!" Jack sat down and told

Yeye everything that had happened. As Jack finished his story, Yeye shook his head in disbelief. "You were lucky this time," he said. "If the Dragon King had made it through the portal—"

Jack shuddered. "I know. That's why we

need to train twice as hard from now on!"

"Oh yeah?" Yeye said in amazement.

"Starting tomorrow." Jack laughed.

Just then he heard his mum calling from indoors. "I'm home! Anyone want pizza?" Jack was suddenly ravenous.

As he went inside, Jack felt the shape of the Jade Coin in his pocket. They might have defeated Yinmei, but the Dragon King was still determined to overthrow the Jade Emperor and take over the Jade Kingdom – and Jack's own world after that. Whatever the Dragon King tried next, Jack and the zodiac animals would be there to stop him!

THE END

Read on for a sneak peek of Jack's next adventure, Tiger Warrior: Rise of the Lion Beast

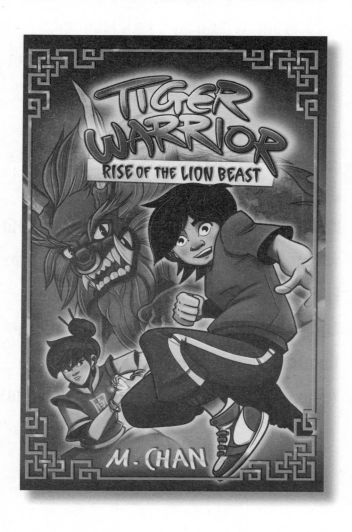

PROLOGUE

The nearby village was filled by bright lights and laughter, but down in the darkness where the land met the ocean, something was stirring. A tall figure glided across the damp sand to the edge of the raging sea, the wind whipping at his scaly cloak. The stranger stopped and faced the dark water in front of him. Flinging back his head, he opened his arms out wide towards the unsettled sea, his razor-sharp nails glinting in the moonlight.

"I am the Dragon King!" he bellowed. "I have returned more powerful than before. And no one shall defeat me!"

He was back. And this time he was going to control the creature that haunted dreams, a legend that every child knew about from the cautionary tales whispered by anxious parents.

The waves crashed into the rocks as the Dragon King held out his clawed hands towards the ocean. He opened his mouth and laughed out loud, his sharp teeth bared menacingly.

"I summon you from the deep – dearest creature of terror, stuff of nightmares! All of the Jade Kingdom will kneel before me when they see that you are under my command!"

Suddenly something came rushing fast towards him beneath the water. A tsunami-like wave was forming; the waves rose high as he lifted his hands into the sky. The Dragon King cackled with glee as the creature zoomed towards him.

"Come, my magnificent and terrifying monster! You may have defeated me twice, Tiger Warrior, but there shall not be a third time! I am still here! And soon you and the whole of the Jade Kingdom will cry in despair as I take over!" boomed the Dragon King, his voice carrying though the sea air.

"Come, Nian! Rise from the deep! Together we shall rule!" he called out.

Three large wooden fishing boats bobbed uneasily on the surface. Then suddenly, one by one, each one was pulled under. Splintered planks rose to the surface and floated on the ocean until they washed up on the waves at the Dragon King's feet.

The dark clouds loomed overhead as the Dragon King's eyes widened. A gigantic, lion-like head was emerging from the waves! It had two huge horns, red eyes, a matted black mane and huge fangs dripping with saliva. The Dragon King took a step back as the creature towered over him, more fierce and more ferocious than his description. "Welcome, Nian." The Dragon King bowed, then produced a glowing jewel from his pocket. "I have a job for you."

With the beast by his side, the Dragon King turned towards the village. His plan was coming together well.

CHAPTER ONE

"Jack, can you grab those bags of oranges from the boot of the car?" his mum asked.

It was Lunar New Year, and they had just arrived at the Chinese Community Centre for a party. There would be lots of families sharing food, a storyteller and even a Lion Dance later on. Jack was really excited – Lunar New Year's Eve was one of his favourite times of the year. He loved the bit where they pretended to eat the lettuce dangling from the doorway. And then to top the celebration off, firecrackers would be let off and Jack and all the other kids would be given money in red envelopes called 'hongbao'. It was one tradition that Jack was especially happy about. *Who wouldn't want an envelope full of money!* Jack thought. He was hoping to save up enough for a new computer game.

"Jack!" Mum said impatiently.

Jack rushed to help. In the realm of the Jade Kingdom, he was the Tiger Warrior, a powerful hero tasked with protecting a magical land – but back in his world he was just a normal boy expected to help his mum by carrying stuff.

"The house is clean, I've bought the decorations and the firecrackers ..." Mum was muttering to herself. Even though Mum wasn't Chinese, she made sure Jack learned about the traditions his father, Ju Long, had celebrated. Now that his dad was no longer alive, it was up to Mum and his grandad, Yeye, to tell Jack about his Chinese heritage.

Jack had always thought that his grandad, Yeye, was just trying to teach him when he told him all the old myths and legends – but really Yeye had a magical secret – he was preparing Jack to become the next Tiger Warrior, like his father and Yeye before him.

The Tiger Warrior was the guardian of a magical world called the Jade Kingdom. Yeye had given him a jade coin with the power of the animals of the zodiac, and with their magical abilities, Jack had to protect the Jade Kingdom. Because every single creature from Chinese myth was real there, and if they destroyed the Jade Kingdom, our world would be next!

Read Tiger Warrior: Rise of the Lion Beast *to find out what happens ...*

WHICH ZODIAC ANIMAL ARE YOU?

*Jack and the other Tiger Warriors are all born in the
year of the Tiger. Use the chart and descriptions
below to work out which zodiac animal you are!
Try it for your family and friends, too!*

ZODIAC ANIMAL	WHAT YEAR WERE YOU BORN IN?									
Rat	1924	1936	1948	1960	1972	1984	1996	2008	2020	2032
Ox	1925	1937	1949	1961	1973	1985	1997	2009	2021	2033
Tiger	1926	1938	1950	1962	1974	1986	1998	2010	2022	2034
Rabbit	1927	1939	1951	1963	1975	1987	1999	2011	2023	2035
Dragon	1928	1940	1952	1964	1976	1988	2000	2012	2024	2036
Snake	1929	1941	1953	1965	1977	1989	2001	2013	2025	2037
Horse	1930	1942	1954	1966	1978	1990	2002	2014	2026	2038
Sheep	1931	1943	1955	1967	1979	1991	2003	2015	2027	2039
Monkey	1932	1944	1956	1968	1980	1992	2004	2016	2028	2040
Rooster	1933	1945	1957	1969	1981	1993	2005	2017	2029	2041
Dog	1934	1946	1958	1970	1982	1994	2006	2018	2030	2042
Pig	1935	1947	1959	1971	1983	1995	2007	2019	2031	2043

WORDSEARCH

Help Jack find all the hidden words in this word search!

JADE FENGHUANG YEYE
DRAGON ZODIAC KING
TIGER WARRIOR PRINCESS

Y	P	G	Y	C	V	I	D	F	Z	D	P	I	H
G	O	R	E	G	W	A	R	R	I	O	R	E	G
V	Y	O	Y	D	N	R	Y	E	Y	I	D	N
G	G	O	E	G	E	O	U	S	L	V	N	A	I
U	D	U	R	E	B	W	E	S	L	R	C	S	K
D	R	O	J	A	D	E	J	F	E	O	E	O	N
W	P	E	O	A	R	U	D	B	O	S	S	Y	I
R	R	D	L	E	A	P	R	D	H	O	S	O	A
O	N	E	L	E	G	E	N	S	D	K	T	O	C
I	O	I	Y	D	O	R	P	M	O	I	I	Y	W
R	U	O	F	E	N	G	H	U	A	N	G	P	Y
R	R	E	E	R	O	E	D	D	I	G	E	O	H
A	Y	D	R	D	B	C	Y	R	L	C	R	R	Y
W	O	O	P	T	H	T	Z	O	D	I	A	C	F

ANIMAL CHARACTERISTICS

RAT

Rats might have a bit of a bad reputation in books and films, but they're number one when it comes to the zodiac. People born in the Year of the Rat are quick-witted, persuasive and very smart. They have excellent taste but can be known to be a little greedy!

OX

The Ox is patient and powerful. People born in this year are known for being kind to others. While they can be a little stubborn, people born in the Year of Ox make the best friends – they can always be counted on to protect the ones that they love.

Tigers are famously strong and majestic, so it's no wonder that Tiger Warriors like Jack and his yeye are born in this year. People born in the Year of the Tiger are courageous but are known to be a bit moody, too!

Forget the cute bunnies, people born in the Year of the Rabbit are the cool kids! Known for being popular, sincere and for always helping others, you're likely to find rabbits at home with lots of guests around.

DRAGON

If you're born in this year, you're very lucky, indeed! The charismatic dragon is revered all over China. Those born in the Year of the Dragon are energetic and fearless, but can be a bit selfish ... No wonder the Dragon King thinks he should be the leader of the Jade Kingdom!

SNAKE

Those born in the Year of the Sssnake are quiet, charming and smart. They're very good with money, but be careful, they're known for getting quite jealous!

People born in the Year of the Horse are very energetic and love to travel. But remember, they do not like waiting. They want to bolt right out of the gates!

HORSE

GOAT

Also known as the Year of the Sheep, people born in this year can be a little shy but are great at understanding people. They're happy to be left alone with their thoughts, and maybe think a bit too much about what others think of them.

MONKEY

Monkeys are a lot of fun to be around. Active and entertaining, people born in this year are great at making people laugh! They like to listen to others but can sometimes lack self-control.

ROOSTER

Hard-working and practical, those born in the Year of the Rooster have a bit of a reputation for being perfectionists. They're very reliable – you can always trust a rooster.

People born in the Year of the Dog are amazing friends and great at sharing. They sometimes get a little moody, but they're famous for being good, honest people.

What a great sign to be in! People born in the Year of the Pig are known for being luxurious! They love learning and helping others.

*For fun activities and more about
Jack and the Jade Kingdom, go to:*

www.orchardseriesbooks.co.uk